Mystery

by Susan Saunders
Illustrated by Eileen Christelow

A Bantam Skylark Book®
Toronto • New York • London • Sydney • Auckland

RL 4, 008–011

MYSTERY CAT

A Bantam Skylark Book/March 1986

Skylark Books is a registered trademark of Bantam Books, Inc.
Registered in U.S. Patent and Trademark Office and elsewhere.

Mystery Cat is a trademark of Cloverdale Press Inc.

Produced by Cloverdale Press Inc.
133 Fifth Avenue
New York, NY 10003

ISBN 0-553-15377-3

Published simultaneously in the United States and Canada

PRINTED IN THE UNITED STATES OF AMERICA

0 9 8 7 6 5 4 3 2 1

Chapter One

It was Samantha who saw him first. He was a big, scruffy, gray cat. He had a notched left ear and a permanent kink in his tail. And he stalked across her yard as though he owned the place.

Samantha raised her head from the lawn where she had been resting. A good-sized dog, Samantha was nonetheless something of a coward. Still, it was *only* a cat.

Samantha lurched to her feet and trailed cautiously after the intruder. But when the gray cat suddenly whirled on her with a low, threatening growl, Samantha did what any sensible dog would do: she retreated and barked for help.

It wasn't long before the screen door leading from the McCoy kitchen to the backyard opened. "Now what?" grumbled Kelly Ann McCoy.

Kelly Ann was usually pretty good-natured. But it was late on Friday afternoon, and she was feeling just a little angry. Her parents were out grocery shopping. Her seven-year-old twin brothers, Michael and Andrew, had been at home with bad colds for two days. Now it was Kelly Ann's job to see that they stayed quietly in bed.

First Andrew and Michael had had a bubble-gum-blowing contest. Kelly Ann had peeled burst bubbles off their chins and out of their eyelashes. Then she had poured each twin a glass of orange juice. Michael had spilled his on the floor and on his bed. Kelly Ann had given him another glass of juice and had changed his sticky sheets. She had changed Andrew's sheets, too, because, as he had explained, "What's the good of being a twin if our sheets don't match?" And her parents hadn't been gone two hours yet!

"Samantha, what's *wrong* with you?" Kelly Ann asked irritably as she rounded the corner of the house. Then she saw the gray cat.

"Bad dog!" she scolded Samantha. "You leave that poor cat alone!"

Samantha's ears twitched, and her feathery tail drooped. Unjustly accused, she whined pitifully. All she wanted to do was crawl inside her doghouse for a relaxing snooze.

Kelly Ann ignored her complaints. "Nice kitty," she said, walking forward slowly so she wouldn't alarm the cat. "Nice kitty." She squatted down a little way from the big gray tom. Before long, the cat was rubbing against her knee, talking to her in a low, rattly purr.

"I haven't seen you around here before," Kelly Ann said. "And you're kind of skinny. I wonder if you belong to anybody?"

Then she heard one of the twins calling her.

She gave the cat a last pat and scrambled to her feet. "Samantha, you leave him alone!" she called over her shoulder as she trotted back to the house.

Misunderstood Samantha gave Kelly Ann's warning the attention it deserved—she flopped down in her doghouse and turned her back on the world.

Kelly Ann broke up a pillow fight in the twins' room and got them settled down again. Then she collapsed in the big chair in the living room. Opening her library book, she was back in the days of chivalry, jousting in a tournament with King Arthur's noble knights Lancelot and Gawain. She was so wrapped up in what she was reading that she didn't understand what her father meant when he said later, "Who's your pal on the back steps?" His mustache curled up at the ends as he smiled down at her.

"Sorry it took us so long," her mother added. "The store was really crowded today. Where are the twins?"

"They're in their room," Kelly Ann answered. "What pal?" she asked her father.

"A tomcat—a beat-up looking gray stray," her father answered. "He wouldn't move—we had to step over him to get through the back door."

"He's still here?" Kelly Ann exclaimed. She leaped to her feet and raced to the back door. Sure enough, there he was, curled up on the doormat with his crooked tail tucked neatly around him.

Mr. McCoy peered at the cat over Kelly Ann's head. "Poor old tough guy," he said. "Looks like he could use a square meal."

"Oh, no, you don't," Kelly Ann's mother said firmly. "Kevin, if we feed him, he'll never leave. And we can't afford another pet right now."

"But, Mom," Kelly Ann pleaded, "I'm sure he'd eat table scraps. Or I could use some of my baby-sitting money to buy cat food." For the past year, Kelly Ann had baby-sat for some of the other families in the neighborhood. "Besides, don't you think I should have first hand experience with as many animals as possible?" Kelly Ann was considering being a vet, and this sounded like a convincing argument to her.

"Well," said Mrs. McCoy, "the gray cat *did* look a little bony." But she added, "He may already belong to someone."

"He's a stray, all right," Mr. McCoy said to his wife. "He didn't get all those battle scars lolling on someone's living room couch. He won't eat much, Eileen. And he probably won't stick around here long, either."

"Kevin, you're worse than Kelly Ann," Mrs. McCoy said, shaking her head and smiling. "All right—but he is not to come into this house under any circumstances. Kelly Ann, you'll have to give him a bath on the first really warm day—he's

4

covered with grease and dirt. And you will have to pay for his food. We just can't stretch our budget any further right now."

Mr. McCoy was a small contractor. He restored old houses, put in new windows, reshingled, and built garages. Recently business had been very slow. Mrs. McCoy was working part-time as a computer programmer at an insurance company. A family of five—plus a dog—can be very expensive.

But Kelly Ann wasn't thinking about that now. She opened the back door and stroked the cat's fur, running her finger over his torn ear.

"I guess you *have* been in lots of battles," she said musingly. "And had plenty of exciting adventures. I think I'll call you Lancelot! Lancelot, wait right here—I'll be back with dinner in a second."

Kelly Ann ran inside and grabbed her wallet. Then she jumped on her bike and pedaled to the Superette, a small grocery store at the end of the street. She had a new pet, a pet with an exciting past who needed her now! Samantha was really her parents' dog. But Lancelot would be entirely Kelly Ann's.

Although the grocery clerk told Kelly Ann that cats were "very particular" about what they ate, Lancelot made a very good meal of moist cat food—a large bag cost only two dollars and twenty-nine cents. And later that evening, he seemed to settle down happily in the box lined with old towels that Kelly Ann fixed for him in a corner of the garage. But when she woke up the next morning, Lancelot was gone.

"Don't be too disappointed," Mrs. McCoy said. "You gave him a good dinner and a comfortable place to rest for a night. Lancelot is probably on his way to his next quest."

But Kelly Ann found herself glancing through the screen door often that day. And all she saw was lazy Samantha, dozing in the May sunlight.

Mr. McCoy had been right when he said Lancelot probably wouldn't stick around long. "I guess I'd better just forget about him," Kelly Ann said sadly to her mother.

The McCoys had sat down to dinner when Samantha started to bark loudly. Kelly Ann's face lit up—could it be. . .?

"Go ahead and take a look," her mother said.

Kelly Ann jumped up from her chair and rushed to the back door. It was starting to get dark outside, so she switched on the porch light. "Lancelot?" she called.

"Mrow!" a voice answered. Two glowing eyes moved toward her through the twilight. Lancelot was back from the wars and ready for dinner.

On Saturday morning, the day after Lancelot had arrived at the McCoys', a gray cat turned up at the Barnetts' house, on the other side of Main

Street. He had a thick neck, a notched left ear, and a permanent kink in his tail.

Unfortunately, he didn't make a good impression on Mrs. Barnett. She had set down a bag from the butcher shop on the steps while she unlocked the back door. Before she could pick up the bag again, the big, scruffy feline had grabbed a package of Mr. Natovsky's special frankfurters between his teeth and raced down the driveway.

"Stop!" Mrs. Barnett shouted in vain.

Hillary Barnett happened to be turning her bike into the driveway at just that moment. "Hey!" she shouted at the cat, cutting the gray thief off before he could make good his escape.

The cat was so startled to find his exit route blocked that he dropped the package. He also stopped running. He walked over to the grass at the edge of the driveway, sat down, and nonchalantly started washing his face.

"Of all the nerve!" Mrs. Barnett said. "Now he's pretending he had nothing to do with it!"

"Glynis"—Hillary always called her mother by her first name—"he's probably really hungry, but he's trying to be cool about it," Hillary said reprovingly. She laid her bike down. Then she picked up the chain of frankfurters, a mixture of ground veal and pork that Mr. Natovsky prepared specially for Mrs. Barnett. Hillary pulled off one of the links and walked over to the cat. "Besides," she said as she fed it to him, "he could have grabbed the fillets."

"I suppose that's true," Mrs. Barnett said. "Oh, there goes the phone!" She picked up the bag and rushed into the house.

Mrs. Barnett wasn't nearly so agreeable when Hillary told her later that she wanted to keep the cat. "But, Hillary," she said, "he's so unattractive. Besides, I'm sure he must belong to *somebody*— although I can't imagine whom," she added, looking at the feline felon doubtfully.

Hillary shook her head. "He acts like he's on his own," she said. "And he doesn't have a collar."

"Then he's bound to have fleas and goodness knows what else," Glynis said. She took another tack. "Mary Watson's Persian just had three kittens. Wouldn't you rather have one of those?"

"This cat may not be exactly beautiful," Hillary said of the gray tom, "but he has a lot of style. And Mary Watson's Persians all look as though they need braces to correct their underbites. Every time I see one of those kittens, I think about what I still have to go through." Hillary had been "wired" with braces for six months.

"I don't have time to argue about it now," said Mrs. Barnett. "I'm already late for the planning committee meeting at the Guild Hall. Speak to your father about it when he gets home. I'll be back for lunch around one o'clock."

Mr. Barnett was a lawyer. If he were in the mood, he could argue about something forever.

"He kind of reminds me of a tomcat my uncle Willie had when I was a little boy," Mr. Barnett said to Hillary later. They were standing at the front window watching the cat sharpen his claws on the birch tree. "He could beat up every cat in town, and half the dogs, too," Mr. Barnett added. "That's an idea," he continued. "Maybe this one will keep other people's dogs out of our yard. What are you going to call him?"

Hillary already had the perfect name for the cat—"Frank," she said. "Short for Frankfurter."

"A good name," said her father. "He was one of the justices of the Supreme Court."

Hillary, of course, meant Mr. Natovsky's frankfurters, not the Supreme Court's. But she nodded knowingly.

"George says I can keep him," Hillary told her mother when she got back from her meeting.

"Oh, all right," said Mrs. Barnett with a sigh.

"But he'll have to go to the vet as soon as we can get an appointment. He needs shots, a complete physical, a bath...everything. And he is not, under any circumstances, ever to come into this house! Mrs. Griffis wouldn't stand for it." Mrs. Griffis was the Barnetts' housekeeper.

"But don't worry about that, Frank," Hillary said later to the cat as she fed him three more frankfurters. "We'll work something out."

Unconcerned, the gray cat washed up, stretched out contentedly on the Barnetts' front steps, and went to sleep.

Frank disappeared in the afternoon. But Hillary's dad reassured her: "Cats have their own business to take care of. He'll be back—where else is he going to eat so well?"

Mr. Barnett was right. That night Hillary had been asleep for several hours when she heard a cat meowing somewhere outside. She jumped out of bed, opened her window, and stuck her head out. There under the streetlamp was Frank —she could just see the kink in his tail.

"Sssst!" Hillary hissed, hoping not to wake up her parents.

The cat trotted right over to her window. She pushed it open even wider, and he leaped onto the sill. Soon he lay at the foot of Hillary's bed on a big feather pillow, his eyes blinking and feet twitching as he dreamed of adventures to come.

Chapter Two

For over a week the big gray cat—because Lancelot and Frank *were* one and the same—lived a double life. He arrived at Kelly Ann's house after she had gotten home from the Windsor Middle School. He stayed for dinner and an early evening nap in the McCoys' garage. Then, after a midnight prowl, he turned up at Hillary's house to spend the rest of the night on the feather pillow. He had breakfast at the Barnetts'. Sometimes he hung around long enough for a quick visit with Hillary when she got home from Lincoln Country Day in the school station wagon. Then it was back to the McCoys' again.

At the McCoys', Lancelot ate moist cat food and seemed to enjoy it. At the Barnetts', the menu was roast pork with rosemary, chicken with walnuts, veal scallops with cream, or whatever else Hillary could talk Mrs. Griffis into contributing from the overstuffed refrigerator.

At the Barnetts', no dog even dared to walk down the sidewalk when Frank was at home. At the McCoys', Lancelot reached an uneasy truce with Samantha—uneasy for Samantha, that is.

As the victor, Lancelot did as he pleased, even going so far as to nap in her doghouse.

All went well until the mothers in both houses decided it was past time for the cat to have his bath. Mrs. McCoy was first. "Kelly Ann," she said when she got home from work one afternoon, "there's a bottle of flea shampoo for Lancelot in my bag."

"But, Mom," Kelly Ann asked worriedly, "do you think it's warm enough to bathe him? It's still pretty cool when the sun goes down. And he wanders all over the place at night. What if he catches cold?"

"We'll close him up in the garage overnight," Mrs. McCoy said, "and keep him there until he's absolutely dry."

She found the plastic washtub she had used to bathe the twins in when they were babies. "You must bathe a cat just as you bathe a dog," she said to her daughter. Kelly Ann agreed—they had bathed Samantha many times. Why should this be that different?

It *was* different. Unlike Samantha, Lancelot minded being bathed—he minded it very much. In fact, he behaved as though Kelly Ann and her mother were trying to drown him. That's where the biggest difference between bathing Lancelot and bathing Samantha became apparent: Lancelot had sixteen very sharp claws.

Even before they had him thoroughly wet

with water from the garden hose, both Mrs. McCoy and Kelly Ann had some pretty good scratches. And Lancelot showed no signs of calming down. He growled continuously from deep in his throat.

"Wow!" said Andrew, very impressed—the twins had run outside to see what was going on.

"He's just like a *tiger*," Michael added.

With his ears laid flat against his head, his long tail thrashing back and forth, and growling his deep, rumbling growl, Lancelot *was* a lot more like a tiger than the gracious cavalier that Kelly Ann imagined him to be. Only Samantha didn't seem surprised—she left the backyard altogether.

"Never mind," Mrs. McCoy said grimly, forcing the cat back down into the washtub. "We're finishing what we started." She and Hillary took turns holding Lancelot down and putting on pairs of Mr. McCoy's work gloves. They squirted the cat with shampoo, lathered it well, left it on for five minutes to take care of any fleas in residence—not an easy job, holding down a furious, soap-covered cat for that long—then rinsed Lancelot off.

"Carry him into the garage," Mrs. McCoy said to Kelly Ann. "I'll close the door behind you."

Kelly Ann wrapped Lancelot up in an old towel and carried him inside. "I'm really sorry," she said to the snarling, squirming cat. "But don't you feel better, now that you're all clean?"

Her answer was an outraged hiss. As soon as she put him down, Lancelot dashed under Mrs. McCoy's old car and refused to come out.

"Just leave him alone for a while," Mrs. McCoy advised. "His humor will improve as he dries off." She closed the garage door again.

But Lancelot didn't emerge from under the car for his evening meal. And when Kelly Ann visited him in the garage the next morning, he hissed at her, his eyes glinting.

"He'll never forgive us for doing this to him," Kelly Ann told her mother. She felt awful about it.

"He'll get over it," Mrs. McCoy said. "But it's kind of chilly and damp this morning. I think he had better stay put until you get home from school."

It was very hard for Kelly Ann to concentrate on her lessons at the Windsor Middle School that day. She kept imagining Lancelot in the dark garage, imprisoned and outraged.

It was even harder for Hillary Barnett. When Frank didn't show up the night before, she hadn't worried too much. She was sure he would turn up for breakfast. But he hadn't. When Hillary got home after school, and the cat still wasn't around, and her mother hadn't seen him all day either, she really began to worry.

"I'm sure he's fine," she said to reassure herself. "He can take care of himself." But she decided she would take a look around the neighborhood on her bike.

This was the Barnetts' first year in Windsor—they had moved there from the city. Hillary's private school was in a neighboring town, so she didn't know any kids to ask about the cat. But after she had ridden around for an hour or so on her bike, she spotted a Windsor police car.

The policeman driving it, Officer Waters, stopped when Hillary waved. "Anything the matter?" he asked.

"I've lost a cat," Hillary said. "Big, gray, with a kink in his tail."

"Have you spoken to the people at the animal shelter?" the policeman asked her.

"No," Hillary said, "I hadn't thought of that. I guess I was afraid something worse might have happened to him...like he got run over...or something," she finished in a low voice.

Officer Waters shook his head. "No," he said, "I haven't seen any sign of that. Call Mrs. Green at the animal shelter—she may have some news for you. And I'll keep an eye open for a cat with a kink in his tail."

Hillary gave him her name and address. Then she rode slowly home. She saw a fat calico on a fence, a striped kitten sleeping on the hood of a car, even a fuzzy white cat on a leash. But no Frank. And the lady at the animal shelter couldn't help her, either. "We haven't taken in any strays at all since the day before yesterday," she told Hillary.

Hillary picked at her dinner. All she could think of was how much Frank would have enjoyed the chicken paprika. She went to bed early, but she couldn't sleep. She tossed and turned, half dozing, half listening for a familiar meow.

Meanwhile, the McCoys had fed Lancelot his dinner. Mrs. McCoy had agreed with Kelly Ann that the cat's fur *had* to be dry by now. So they opened the garage door. Lancelot bolted through the door and into the night. Kelly Ann had a terrible feeling that she would never see him again.

Hillary Barnett had just fallen into an uneasy sleep when she awoke with a start. A cat was yowling outside her window—it was Frank!

He was curled up on Hillary's bed in less than a minute, looking a little fluffier than usual. And he smelled kind of funny, too.

"Poor guy," Hillary mumbled, just before she fell asleep again herself. "He's back just in time for his appointment at the vet's tomorrow."

Chapter Three

The next day, it was Kelly Ann's turn to worry. Lancelot didn't come home in the afternoon. Nor was he there for dinner. Before she went to bed, Kelly Ann checked the cardboard box where he slept in the garage. Empty. He didn't even reappear the next afternoon.

Kelly Ann called the animal shelter—she knew about it because one of the people who worked there had visited her sixth-grade class. But the man who answered the phone told her the only cat they had taken in all week was a black-and-white female.

"I don't suppose you'd be interested in adopting her?" he asked hopefully. Kelly Ann wasn't—she just wanted Lancelot back.

The cat didn't come home that night, either. The following day, Saturday, was so warm it felt like summer. But Kelly Ann had no desire to go outside—everything reminded her of Lancelot: the garage, the back steps, even Samantha.

"It's not going to help moping around here all day," Mrs. McCoy told her. "Why don't you go over to the police station? They found Samantha for us when she followed that boy home after school. Maybe they've seen Lancelot."

"All right," Kelly Ann said tonelessly. She dragged herself out to her bike. But she knew it was useless. She was convinced—after his enforced bath and being locked up in the garage—that Lancelot no longer trusted the McCoys. He was *never* coming back.

Early that same morning, Mrs. Barnett and Hillary brought Frank home from the veterinarian. He had gotten all of his shots. Since the vet was fairly certain that Frank had never been vaccinated, he had boarded him for a couple of days "for observation." "Once in a while, an unvaccinated cat has a dangerously strong reaction to the serum," the vet had explained to Hillary.

But the only strong reaction Frank had was to going to the vet's in the first place. He hissed all the way there and growled all the way back. In between the two car trips, he had been bathed, dusted with flea powder, and his ears had been swabbed. Even his teeth had been cleaned.

"I don't know that there's much of an improvement," Mrs. Barnett said, as Hillary let the cat out of the carrier in front of a plate full of Mr. Natovsky's special frankfurters.

"I think he looks elegant," Hillary said. "Especially when he smiles." Frank's white-fanged smile was really more of a yawn. It was followed almost immediately by a nap in the sun.

Hillary went for a bike ride while Frank rested. When she ended up near the police station, she decided to leave a message for Officer Waters: "The Barnetts' cat came home."

And that's how Hillary Barnett and Kelly Ann McCoy found themselves at the Windsor Police Station at the same time.

Hillary walked in to leave her message just in time to hear Kelly Ann's description of her missing cat: "He's tall for a cat," Kelly Ann was saying to the policeman at the front desk. "He's gray. He has a piece missing out of one ear. And his tail is unusual—it has a bend near the end."

"That's my cat Frank you're talking about," Hillary said, sizing up the girl in front of her. She looked about eleven—Hillary's age—with long blond hair.

"He's *my* cat, and his name is Lancelot," Kelly Ann replied firmly. Facing her was a girl with short, dark hair and braces on her teeth. "Private school rich kid," Kelly Ann said to herself, for two reasons: one, the girl was about Kelly Ann's age and she had never seen her before, although there was only one middle school in Windsor; two, she was wearing a T-shirt that said, "Ski Sun Valley." Just to *get* to Sun Valley, Idaho, from Windsor would cost a lot of money.

"Which ear is the piece missing from?" the private school rich kid quizzed her.

"The left ear," said Kelly Ann McCoy.

"Then it's *my* cat," said Hillary Barnett. "His name is Frank, and he's asleep on *my* front steps."

"Since *when* is he *your* cat?" Kelly Ann wanted to know. "He eats dinner at *my* house every evening and sleeps in *my* garage!"

"He sleeps on *my* bed," Hillary responded angrily. "And eats breakfast in *my* backyard. And waits for *me* after school!"

"Ladies, ladies," interrupted the listening policeman. "This is probably a case of mistaken identity. Why don't you both describe your cats again? You first," he said to Kelly Ann.

"My cat, *Lancelot*, is a tall, gray cat," she began again. "He has a notched left ear and a kink in his tail and—"

Two patrolmen were signing in. "Hey," one of them said, "that sounds like old M.C." He turned to his partner. "You remember him—wherever the action was, that's where we'd see M.C."

"M.C.?" said Hillary.

"For Mystery Cat," the partner explained. "We never figured out where he was coming from, or where he was going. But he seemed to have a sixth sense for trouble. He turned up at every traffic jam, fire, and arrest. He was even at last year's bank robbery. We were beginning to think he had a handle on every crime in Windsor. But he hasn't been around for a while."

"That's because he's been at my house," said Hillary.

"Or mine," added Kelly Ann.

"Mystery Cat," Hillary said. "It isn't as good a name as Frank, but it's a lot better than *Lance-ce-lot*." She rolled her eyes as she pronounced the name.

But Kelly Ann didn't take her up on it. "Mystery Cat," she repeated. "It sounds romantic, like Robin Hood...or the Scarlet Pimpernel."

"The Scarlet Pimpernel?" Hillary snorted. "What kind of weird name is that?"

"It's from a book!" Kelly Ann quickly let her know.

"Oh," Hillary said. The last book she'd read was about undersea adventures in a minisub, and the one before that an account of the first women's team to scale Mount Everest.

Kelly Ann glared at Hillary. But before she could open her mouth, the policeman at the desk interjected, "There's a cat at this young lady's house"—pointing at Hillary—"who *sounds* like your cat. But I suggest that you go to her house and take a look at him. It may be another animal altogether."

One of the patrolmen added, "If it is M.C.— and it sure sounds like him—you may as well share him, because *nobody* owns that cat."

Kelly Ann looked at Hillary. Hillary shrugged her shoulders. "Why not?" she said. "Let's go."

Kelly Ann followed Hillary down the steps, and they both climbed on their bikes. "Which way?" Kelly Ann asked.

"Around the corner to the left, then straight ahead," Hillary answered.

That was the way to Brentwood—some of the biggest houses were in that part of town. And when Hillary turned her bike into the pebbled driveway of a huge modern house, all Kelly Ann could say was, "Wow!" The McCoys' little two-story home would fit in it twice and have room left over.

But Hillary misunderstood. "Yeah," she answered, "gross, isn't it? I'm going to be an architect. And I'm planning to build everything out of logs." Then she pointed: "There he is. On the front steps."

"Lancelot!" Kelly Ann shouted. She dropped her bike and ran across the lawn to the front steps. She scooped up the gray cat and squeezed him against her. To Hillary she said, "I thought I was never going to see him again. He really hated us for giving him a bath."

"*You* bathed him?" Hillary burst out laughing. "We bathed him, too, or at least the vet did. We even had his teeth cleaned. Frank is definitely the cleanest cat in Windsor."

The girls' eyes met when Hillary said "Frank." Kelly Ann was still hugging the cat to her, and he was purring loudly. "Mystery Cat," Kelly Ann corrected. "M.C."

"Right," Hillary agreed. "M.C."

Chapter Four

M.C., the object of all this attention, squirmed to be put down. Then he washed up, stretched, and headed down the driveway. The girls watched him cross the street and cut across a neighboring yard.

"I wonder where he's going?" Kelly Ann asked.

"He comes to your house in the afternoon, doesn't he?" Hillary answered. "He's probably on his way."

"Afternoon!" Kelly Ann looked at her watch. "I'm going to be late for lunch!" She picked up her bike. "Oh, by the way," she said, "I'm Kelly Ann McCoy." She stuck out her hand.

"Hillary Barnett," said Hillary, shaking Kelly Ann's hand enthusiastically.

"I'm glad we got this straightened out," Kelly Ann said.

"Me, too," said Hillary. "It's been nice meeting you."

"Maybe we'll get together again sometime," Kelly Ann said. "See you..." She glided slowly down the driveway on her bike, her feet off the pedals. Then she braked to a stop and turned around. Hillary was standing in the driveway looking the tiniest bit wistful. "...Unless you'd like to come to my house for lunch?" Kelly Ann called back.

Hillary didn't hesitate. "Great!" she said. "I'll leave a note for George and Glynis."

"George and Glynis?" said Kelly Ann.

"My parents," Hillary explained and dashed inside the house.

Kelly Ann tried to imagine herself calling her father and mother Kevin and Eileen. But she couldn't. Obviously, things were done differently in Brentwood.

Differently, but judging from Hillary's reactions, not necessarily better. For example, Hillary loved Kelly Ann's house. "It's like the house in *Hansel and Gretel*," she said, as they braked their bikes in front.

Kelly Ann laughed. "As a matter of fact," she said, "that carved stuff around the roof is even called gingerbread. But it's kind of small for the five of us. And a dog."

"Five? You have brothers and sisters?" Hillary asked.

"Brothers. Seven years old. Twins," Kelly Ann added. "But not identical."

"Twins! Neat!" said Hillary. "I always wanted to be a twin. I'm an only child," she added.

"That would be a nice change sometimes,"

said Kelly Ann with a grin.

"Twins. And a dog," Hillary said thoughtfully. "We lived in an apartment in the city until last year. I had fish and turtles and once a gerbil. But M.C. is my first real pet."

"You lived in the city?" said Kelly Ann. "Did you like it?"

"A lot," Hillary answered. "There's always something to do there."

Before Kelly Ann could ask her anything else, Andrew and Michael burst around the side of the house. Samantha was right behind them.

"Did you find him? Is Lancelot coming back?" Michael asked. "Did he get run over?" Andrew shouted. Samantha put dirty paws on Hillary's T-shirt and gazed searchingly into her eyes.

Kelly Ann sorted them out for Hillary. "The redheaded one is Andrew," she said.

"I'm older," Andrew told Hillary.

"By about five minutes," his sister retorted. "And this is Michael." Michael had brown hair and long black eyelashes.

"Guys," Kelly Ann said, "this is Hillary Barnett. Oh, and the one with spots," she added, "is Samantha."

Mrs. McCoy opened the front door and stuck her head out. "I wondered what all the noise was about," she said.

"Mom, this is Hillary Barnett. I've asked her to lunch," Kelly Ann told her mother.

"Hello, Hillary," said Mrs. McCoy. She had a pleasant face and blond hair almost the same shade as Kelly Ann's. "Glad you could come. I hope you like tuna sandwiches and deviled eggs."

Kelly Ann thought Hillary was probably used to much fancier stuff. But Hillary spoke right up. "It's my favorite kind of lunch," she said. The girls and the twins trooped into the house and sat down at the big round table in the kitchen.

"Where's Dad?" Kelly Ann asked.

"He's still working on Mr. Whitcomb's skylights," her mother said. "Andrew, pass Hillary the sandwiches. Kelly Ann, you're certainly in better spirits than you were when you left this morning. You must have some good news about Lancelot."

"M.C." Both girls corrected her at once, then laughed.

"That's how I met Hillary," Kelly Ann explained. "At the police station, I was giving a description of *my* lost cat, Lancelot, when Hillary said it sounded just like *her* cat, Frank."

"We were both right," Hillary continued. "He comes here for dinner, then goes to my house for breakfast."

"And it turns out he already has a name: M.C., which stands for Mystery Cat." Kelly Ann took up the story again. "Some of the patrolmen call him that because he mysteriously turns up—

27

at fires and traffic jams and stuff."

Mrs. McCoy laughed. "It all sounds very complicated. And *very* mysterious."

A car turned into the driveway and stopped. Someone ran up the back steps and opened the screen door. "Kelly Ann"—it was Mr. McCoy—"I just saw Lancelot, trotting past the Whitcombs' house. By the time I climbed down from the roof, he had disappeared. But at least we know he's all right."

Then Kelly Ann and Hillary had to retell the whole story for Mr. McCoy's benefit. Just as they finished, Samantha started to bark in the backyard.

"I bet it's M.C.," Kelly Ann said to Hillary. Sure enough, it was. The family watched out the back door as M.C. drank water from Samantha's dish. Then he strolled into her doghouse, sat down, and gave them all a white-fanged yawn. There was a streak of oil down one side of his head. Bits of sawdust clung to his back. M.C. was no longer the cleanest cat in Windsor. Everything was back to normal.

Chapter Five

So the Mystery Cat divided his time between the McCoys and the Barnetts. And Kelly Ann and Hillary spent more and more of *their* time together.

The Barnetts liked Kelly Ann very much. "Such a nice girl," Mrs. Barnett told Hillary. "And such nice manners."

The McCoys felt that Hillary was good for Kelly Ann as well. Although they thought it was wonderful that Kelly Ann liked to read so much, it was good to see her out and doing things with Hillary. "She brings Kelly Ann back down to earth," was the way Mr. McCoy put it.

Suddenly it was the middle of June. School had been over for eight days. Hillary was already worrying about running out of things to do in Windsor.

"I won't be going to camp for four weeks," she said to Kelly Ann. They were lying near the garden in the McCoys' backyard, "cultivating a tan," as Hillary put it. "That's a lot of hours to fill," she went on. "What do people *do* in Windsor in the summertime?"

Kelly Ann so rarely had empty hours that she didn't know what to say. There were the twins to keep an eye on. She checked as many books as she could out of the library and read them one after another. There was a park two blocks away, with a public swimming pool and several baseball diamonds—sometimes some of the neighborhood kids got a game going. And in the afternoons there was M.C., of course.

Almost as if Hillary had read her mind, she asked Kelly Ann, "Where *is* M.C.?"

"I think he and the twins are playing 'fetch' on the front sidewalk," Kelly Ann told her.

"Andrew and Michael taught M.C. to fetch?" asked a disbelieving Hillary.

"I think it's more like M.C. taught the twins," Kelly Ann said with a giggle. "Come on. I'll show you."

Andrew was holding a small, balled-up piece of paper. He rolled it back and forth between his hands for a second.

"M.C. likes the crinkly noise," Michael explained.

M.C. stood motionless, poised halfway down the sidewalk. His ears were pointing straight forward. His eyes were riveted on the paper ball. His crooked tail flicked with excitement.

"Ready, M.C.?" Andrew said. He raised his hand over his head and threw the paper ball as far as he could across the lawn.

M.C. was after it like a shot. He batted it around on the grass a few times. Then he snatched the paper ball between his teeth and trotted back to the twins.

The expression on his face was so self-satisfied that the girls burst out laughing. M.C. ignored them—this was serious business—and dropped the paper ball at Michael's feet.

"He always takes turns," Andrew said.

"I think it's because he knows the game will last longer if he divides it between the two of them," Kelly Ann whispered to Hillary.

"When he wants to play, he even brings the paper himself," Michael said.

Hillary raised her eyebrows.

"It's true," Kelly Ann confirmed. "He must pull it out of trash cans or something."

"M.C. is one smart cat," Hillary said. "He fetches. *And* he provides his own ball."

"When he feels like it," Kelly Ann interposed.

"He even opens doors at my house," Hillary went on.

"Our house, too," Kelly Ann said. "Yesterday I found him inside the house, asleep on my parents' bed! Good thing Mom wasn't home—she would have had a fit!"

"Kelly Ann," Mrs. McCoy called from inside the house, "would you mind riding to the Superette and buying a half-gallon of milk? We're just not going to make it through till Saturday."

"Sure, Mom," Kelly Ann said. She went inside for some money.

"There's a ten-dollar bill in the bedroom," her mother told her. "I think it's on the dresser."

But as soon as Kelly Ann walked through the door, she saw the crumpled bill lying on the floor next to the bed. A breeze from the open window must have blown it off the dresser. Kelly Ann picked it up and pressed it flat against her knee. Then she folded it in half and stuck it in the pocket of her shorts.

"Got it, Mom," she said. "I'll be right back."

"Thanks," said Mrs. McCoy. "And why don't you buy a quart of ice cream for you and Hillary and the boys?" she suggested.

"Okay," Kelly Ann said. "What kind of ice cream do you like?" she asked Hillary when she got outside.

"Mmmm." Hillary thought. "Today, strawberry," she answered.

"Me, too," said Andrew.

"Yeah," said Michael.

They were sitting on the front lawn with Hillary now. M.C. was sprawled out in the shade of a bush, panting a little after his game.

"I'll go with you," Hillary told Kelly Ann.

Mr. Stefanos, the owner of the Superette, was behind the cash register. "Hello, girls," he said. "Hot day."

As he was ringing up the milk and the ice cream, Hillary called to Kelly Ann: "Hey, check out the neat bathing suit on the cover of this magazine."

Kelly Ann handed Mr. Stefanos the ten-dollar bill from her pocket and joined Hillary. "I think I'd like it better in blue," she said.

"No, I'd want it just like this," Hillary declared.

"A-hem-m-m!" Mr. Stefanos cleared his throat loudly.

Both girls turned to look at him. "I'm sorry," he said to Kelly Ann, "but I can't accept this." He waved the ten-dollar bill in the air.

"Why not?" asked Kelly Ann. She couldn't imagine what he meant.

"It's funny money," Mr. Stefanos answered. "You know—counterfeit. No good."

Kelly Ann and Hillary looked at each other and back at Mr. Stefanos. "Counterfeit?" Kelly Ann repeated. Her face was starting to feel hot.

"And not very good counterfeit," Mr. Stefanos said. "Look at this."

Kelly Ann and Hillary walked over to the register.

"See here?" Mr. Stefanos poked the ten-dollar bill. "The little points around the Federal Reserve seal—some of them are broken. And the scrollwork on this end is smudged." Holding one end of the bill in each hand, he snapped it a couple of times. "Paper's pretty good. But all in all," he said, "funny money. As they say, not worth the paper it's printed on. Have any idea where it came from?"

"Off the floor in my parents' bedroom," Kelly Ann thought. But that wasn't what Mr. Stefanos meant. Kelly Ann shook her head.

"Well, take it home to show your mother. Take the groceries, too. You can pay me the next time you're in."

"Thanks," Kelly Ann said. She folded the counterfeit bill and stuck it back in her pocket. "Let's go," she said to Hillary.

When they got outside, she whispered, "How weird. And how embarrassing."

"Yeah, I know," Hillary said. "Your face is kind of red. But *you're* not the counterfeiter."

"I know," replied Kelly Ann. "But still. . ."

When the girls got back to the house, Kelly Ann felt even funnier. Her mother met them at the door. "Mr. Stefanos must have given you credit," she guessed. "I thought you said you'd taken the money, but it was still on the dresser." She held out a ten-dollar bill. "Do you want to run this down to the Superette while I dish up the ice cream?"

"But what about *this* ten-dollar bill?" Kelly Ann asked, pulling the "funny money" out of her pocket. "I found it on the floor in your bedroom."

"Our bedroom?" Mrs. McCoy repeated.

"That can't be right. Let me think. . . .I withdrew twenty-five dollars yesterday because I had only a few dollars left in my wallet. Last night I gave one ten-dollar bill to your father. And I left this ten and the rest of the money on the dresser. It's still there." Mrs. McCoy took Kelly Ann's ten-dollar bill. "Where could this have come from?"

"I don't know," Kelly Ann said.

"But don't try to spend it," warned Hillary.

"What?" said Mrs. McCoy.

"Hillary will explain," Kelly Ann told her. She was off to Mr. Stefanos's grocery again.

She puzzled about it on her way to the Superette and back. In the McCoy household, every penny—or at least every dime—was accounted for. Of course her mother would know exactly how much money she had. So how had the counterfeit bill gotten into the McCoys' house?

The plot thickened at the Barnetts' that night at dinner. Hillary had been ready to launch into her tale of the counterfeit bill, when Mrs. Barnett told a story of her own.

"The *most* embarrassing thing happened to me today," she announced.

"For Glynis," Hillary thought, "that could mean anything from running into someone she knows without her hair absolutely perfect to forgetting a word in French."

She poked at the food on her plate waiting

for her turn to talk. She wasn't really following the conversation—until she heard her mother say, "Then I handed the sales clerk thirty dollars —a twenty and a ten-dollar bill."

Now Hillary sat straight up, and her ears practically twitched. "Yes?" she prompted, trying to hurry her mother along to the point of the story.

"The clerk took the money and the scarf I wanted back to the register," Mrs. Barnett went on. "The next thing I knew, she and another salesperson were whispering together and *staring* at me! I asked if there was a problem, and one of them came over to me and said that my money was no good. Well, of course I told her my money is as good as anyone else's. But she gave me a funny look, and told me that one of the bills was counterfeit! Can you imagine?" Glynis said to Mr. Barnett and Hillary. "They seemed to think that I was trying to pass a counterfeit ten-dollar bill! I felt like a criminal!"

Hillary could imagine very well. Glynis was still talking a mile a minute to George. But Hillary's thoughts were elsewhere. She was sure there couldn't be a counterfeit ten-dollar bill in every house in Windsor. So wasn't it almost too much of a coincidence that one had turned up at the McCoys'. . .and one at the Barnetts'?

Hillary decided not to tell her parents her story. She wanted to talk with Kelly Ann first.

Chapter Six

Kelly Ann was barely out of bed the next morning when the phone rang. She picked it up to hear Hillary's voice: "I wanted to call you last night. But George was waiting for a business call, so I couldn't use the phone."

"Anything wrong?" Kelly Ann asked.

"No—but a very interesting thing happened to Glynis yesterday," Hillary answered. "Can you come over? I'd like to show you something."

"Let me ask. Hey, Mom," Kelly Ann called, "may I go over to Hillary's?"

"If you're back by twelve," her mother answered. "I'm going in to work this afternoon for a few hours, and I need you for the twins."

"I'll be right over," Kelly Ann said into the phone. She hung up and pulled on her clothes as fast as she could.

"How about some breakfast?" Mrs. McCoy asked as Kelly Ann dashed through the house.

"No, thanks," she called back on her way out the door. "Not hungry."

Mrs. Barnett was leaving just as Kelly Ann arrived. "Why, hello, Kelly Ann," she said. "How are you, dear?"

"Fine, thank you," Kelly Ann answered.

"Mrs. Griffis has the day off—let yourself in," Mrs. Barnett said. "I think Hillary's in her room."

Mrs. Barnett climbed into her car and backed down the driveway.

"I'm on my way to a meeting," she called. "See you later!"

Hillary *was* in her room. So was M.C., lying on his back on a pillow at the end of Hillary's bed, sound asleep. He opened one eye when Kelly Ann plopped down on the bed next to him. M.C. made a squeaky complaining noise about being disturbed and closed his eye again.

Kelly Ann laughed. "Well, excu-u-use me!" she said to the cat. "Anyway, I thought you weren't supposed to be in the house."

"He's not," Hillary said. "But Glynis and George think I'm entitled to privacy, so they never come down here without calling out first. Which gives me time to boost M.C. out the window." Hillary's eyes were shining with excitement.

"So, what's up?" Kelly Ann asked her. "What happened to your mother yesterday?"

"Glynis tried to spend a counterfeit ten-dollar bill, too!"

"You're kidding!" Kelly Ann said. A counterfeit ten at the McCoys'. And a counterfeit ten at the Barnetts', on the other side of town?

"Almost too much of a coincidence, right?"

Hillary said.

"It's possible," Kelly Ann said slowly, "that *your* mother got her counterfeit bill in change from a store. But *my* mother didn't."

"There's something else," Hillary told her. "Glynis yelled at me this morning for being careless with my allowance. She said Mrs. Griffis found a ten-dollar bill on the living room floor when she was cleaning yesterday."

"You get a ten-dollar allowance?" Kelly Ann was astonished. For the McCoy children, ten-dollar bills were only for special occasions, like birthdays.

"Oh, it's just supposed to teach me how to manage my own money," Hillary said quickly, shrugging it off.

"What did Mrs. Griffis do with the bill?" Kelly Ann asked.

"Gave it to Glynis, and Glynis stuck it in her wallet," Hillary said. "That was the bill she tried to spend. But it wasn't *my* ten-dollar bill. I'd already used mine to buy a ball with a bell in it for M.C., and gotten change."

"Does he like it?" Kelly Ann asked, changing the subject for a moment.

"Not as well as he likes paper balls," Hillary answered. "Which brings us to the point."

"What point?" Kelly Ann said, feeling hopelessly confused.

"Besides counterfeit ten-dollar bills, what do

our families have in common?" asked Hillary.

The girls looked at one another. Then at the same time their heads turned, and they both stared at the same thing—M.C. He was still on his back with his feet in the air and his paws crossed on his chest. He was starting to snore.

"But—" Kelly Ann began.

"Wait a minute," Hillary interrupted, "until I show you Glynis's counterfeit ten-dollar bill. It's in the grapevine basket in the kitchen—everything ends up there sooner or later."

Hillary ran down the hall and was soon back with the bill. She smoothed it out on her desk. "Look," she said. "The points around the seal are broken, just as they were on yours. And it's smudgy on the same end."

"It's wrong in exactly the same places!" Kelly Ann exclaimed.

"Right, which must mean that the two bills were made by the same counterfeiter. I'll bet he threw them out because they weren't any good— maybe when he was just getting started."

"Y-e-e-s," Kelly Ann said, thinking about it.

"Now, what did you tell me just yesterday that M.C. pulls out of trash cans?"

"Crinkly pieces of paper—to play fetch," Kelly Ann said.

"Then," said Hillary, sounding more and more like her lawyer father, "isn't it possible that on his way back and forth from your house to mine, M.C. climbed into a trash can and pulled the funny money out of it?"

"My bill was pretty wrinkled up," Kelly Ann said. "Maybe it *was* thrown out."

"Ah ha!" said Hillary. "So was Glynis's." She pointed to the bill lying on her desk. "You said you found M.C. asleep on your parents' bed two days ago, so we know he's been in their bedroom. And he's always coming into our house. I submit that M.C. picked up one wadded-up bill on his way here and dropped it in this house. And he picked up one on his way to your house and dropped it there. Ladies and gentleman," she said, looking at M.C., "I rest my case."

M.C.'s eyelids had fluttered when he heard his name. He certainly didn't look like a cat mixed up in a mystery.

"The police did say he seemed to have a sixth sense about crime," Kelly Ann recalled.

"So," said Hillary, "all we have to do now is let him show us where he got the bills."

"Why don't we just go to the police?" Kelly Ann asked.

"Why would they pay any attention to us? And do you really think we can convince them to follow a cat around for days, hoping he'll lead them to something?" Hillary asked scornfully. "No, that's what *we're* going to do! Then we'll see about going to the police."

Chapter Seven

"**P**retty soon M.C. will head for your house," Hillary said. "We'd better be ready to trail him, because somewhere between here and there there's a genuine counterfeiter."

"Maybe we shouldn't do this. Maybe it's too dangerous," Kelly Ann said.

"Counterfeiters don't have guns," Hillary scoffed. "They have printing presses."

Suddenly M.C. opened his eyes and sat up. He stretched and yawned, his rough pink tongue curling over his front teeth. Then he stalked across the bed to the window.

"This is it!" Hillary said to Kelly Ann.

M.C. tapped on the window with his front paw. "Mrow!" he demanded. Hillary pushed the window open wider. M.C. jumped down onto the Barnetts' lawn.

"Our bikes—hurry!" Hillary shrieked. The girls raced down the hall and out of the house. They jumped on their bicycles.

"Where is he?" Kelly Ann asked breathlessly.

Hillary peered up and down the empty street. She slammed her fist down on the handlebars of her bike. "We've lost him already!"

But Kelly Ann looked behind them. "There he is, right next to your front steps!"

M.C. had collapsed in the sunshine.

"Great, M.C.," Hillary said. "You're really off to a good start as a crime-buster." She climbed off her bike and sat down on the curb. "This may take awhile," she declared.

So the girls sat and waited for the Mystery Cat to make his move. And waited. . .while M.C. napped a little more, washed himself from the ends of his whiskers to the tip of his crooked tail, and pounced on a leaf.

"I think he's trying to bore us to death so we won't follow him," Hillary decided.

Kelly Ann giggled. But perhaps Hillary was right—because, when they least expected it, M.C. darted across the street and cut through a yard.

"I know this neighborhood better than you do," Hillary said, "so I'll follow him. Take the bikes around to the next street over. Meet you there!" Then she raced after the gray cat.

M.C. slipped through a hedge, and there was nothing for Hillary to do but follow him. The branches tugged at her hair and scratched her arms and legs as she pushed through. "Agh! Ouch! Thanks a lot, M.C.!" Hillary shouted.

When she emerged on the other side of the bushes, M.C. was nowhere in sight. But Hillary wasn't exactly alone. A woman wearing a pink dress and sneakers and holding a garden trowel was glaring at her disapprovingly.

"Just talking to my cat," Hillary said. "Did you see him? Gray, notched ear, kinked tail?"

The woman pointed with her trowel across the yard to the alley beyond. "Great gallumphing oaf crushed my coreopsis and mashed my mimulus!" she fumed.

"Thanks very much," Hillary said.

"Just stay away from my roses!"

It was the first thing she had said that Hillary could understand, and she was pleased to oblige.

The narrow alleys seemed more promising. There was a long row of aluminum trash cans. But when Hillary looked them over, she discovered all the lids were tied on.

"M.C. is a clever cat," Hillary said to herself, "but not even he could pull any paper balls out of these." She sprinted to the end of the alley and beckoned to Kelly Ann. Kelly Ann was riding her own bike and pulling Hillary's along beside her.

"Did you see him?" Hillary asked.

Kelly Ann nodded. "He ran along the top of that high stone fence before he disappeared behind the house over there."

"Well, at least I don't have to do that," Hillary said. "*I* can open the gate."

She lifted the wrought-iron latch on a heavy wooden gate. "I'll meet you on the next street," she turned to tell Kelly Ann.

"Close it!" Kelly Ann screamed.

Hillary whirled to see a big German shepherd hurtling toward her with its long white teeth flashing. She slammed the gate closed and latched it just before the dog reached her. He never barked. But he threw his body against the wooden gate again and again.

"Whew!" Hillary said. "It's a good thing M.C. has nine lives. He's probably already used up a bunch of them just commuting from my house to yours and back. Let's get out of here!"

The girls circled the block, with no luck. "He's definitely given us the slip," Hillary said. "If only we could see over these houses and trees."

Kelly Ann pointed to a pine tree on the next block. "What about climbing that?" she asked.

"I'll do it!" Hillary volunteered.

They started to climb. The lowest branches of the pine were no more than three feet from the ground. The higher branches were spaced about every two feet, all the way up the straight trunk. It was as easy as climbing a ladder.

"On a clear day, I'll bet you can see all the way to the city from up here," Kelly Ann said as they neared the top. The pine began to sway back and forth in the wind. Back and forth...

"It's like being in a boat!" said Kelly Ann.

Then she noticed Hillary wasn't saying anything. "Is something wrong?" Kelly Ann asked.

Hillary gave her a weak smile. "No...noth-

47

ing...It's just that I'm very prone to motion sickness." She clambered down the tree half as fast as she had come up. "Stay up there...I'll just have to sit still for a minute...look for M.C.," a weak voice called up to Kelly Ann.

Kelly Ann scanned the area. At last she saw something promising. Four or five blocks away, behind a pizzeria, she saw a woman bending over a big gray cat.

"I see a gray cat," she called down to Hillary. "But I can't tell from here if it's M.C. or not."

"Let's ride over and take a look." Hillary was feeling better.

The cat at the pizzeria was *not* M.C. He had a white foot. And two whole ears. "Crooked tail and notched ear?" the woman asked. She served her gray cat a bowl of noodles with meat sauce. "I know him. He's a bad character. He used to come around the pizzeria, but we had to run him off. He picked awful fights with Henry here. Try the yellow house one block over. There's an old man there—Brown—who feeds strays."

"The Pirate!" old Mr. Brown exclaimed when the girls had described M.C. "What a swashbuckler! He used to be one of my regular customers. But I haven't seen him in weeks. I was afraid that something had happened to him, with all these unleashed dogs running around, and bad drivers in fast cars." He glanced at his watch. "Excuse me," he said, "but it's time for lunch."

Mr. Brown tore open a huge bag of dry food. Cats materialized out of bushes, from behind the steps, under cars, on top of the porch: short ones, tall ones, smooth haired and fluffy, spry kittens and slow-moving oldsters. But not M.C.

"We were right here," Hillary pointed out, "standing on top of all these cats, and we never even saw one of them. I don't know why I ever thought we could tail M.C. if he wanted to make himself scarce. We may as well forget it!" She sounded completely discouraged.

"We should stop for now, anyway," Kelly Ann said. "I promised I'd be home by noon."

The girls thanked Mr. Brown for the information. Then Hillary said, "I'm going home. Talk to you later." She rode slowly away on her bike.

That afternoon M.C. arrived on schedule at Kelly Ann's. He and the twins had an exciting game of fetch—with regular paper this time. Kelly Ann looked at it carefully: it was part of a take-out menu from a restaurant. Then M.C. lay in the shade and watched the twins play with the walkie-talkies their uncle Rob had sent them.

M.C. cocked his head and looked so puzzled at hearing Andrew's voice come out of a black box that Kelly Ann had to laugh.

But she didn't hear from Hillary. "I wonder if she has a new plan?" Kelly Ann said to herself, because Kelly Ann was beginning to have some ideas of her own.

Chapter Eight

The next morning, Kelly Ann called Hillary. "Are you ready to try again?" she asked her friend.

"There must be hundreds of houses between your place and mine," Hillary said glumly. "Do you know how long it would take us to check them all out? Because M.C.'s certainly no help. I think we've ruined him as a crime-buster."

M.C. was blissfully asleep on Hillary's bed. Hillary poked the big cat with her toe, and he wriggled out of the way without even opening his eyes.

"Good food and easy living," Hillary grumbled, "add up to no more mystery about *this* cat."

"Well, I have a plan," Kelly Ann told her.

"What is it?" Hillary asked, perking up.

"You'll have to come over here. Mom had to take Michael to the doctor," Kelly Ann said. "He fell on a nail playing at Billy's"—Billy Johnson lived next door—"and had to have a shot. So I've got Andrew."

"Be right there," Hillary said and hung up.

At the McCoys', she found Andrew and

Samantha sitting on the front steps. Samantha wagged her tail enthusiastically when she saw Hillary. But Andrew was looking downcast. He was holding two small, black walkie-talkies.

"What's the matter?" Hillary asked him.

"Nobody to talk to," Andrew said, showing her the walkie-talkies.

"I'm in here!" Kelly Ann called from inside the house.

"Tell you what," Hillary said to Andrew. "Give me one of them, and I'll talk to you as soon as I'm finished with Kelly Ann."

"Okay." Andrew handed her a walkie-talkie, although he didn't look as though he thought it would be as much fun as talking to Michael.

Kelly Ann was sitting at the kitchen table, studying a large dark-green-and-white map.

"Are we going away and forgetting about the whole thing?" Hillary asked with a smile.

"This map could be just what we need to track down the counterfeiter," Kelly Ann said coolly. Before Hillary could ask any questions, Kelly Ann continued, "But first, what would you say M.C. likes to do best?"

That was easy. "Sleep," Hillary answered. "Or eat."

"Right," said Kelly Ann. "Now, he does his sleeping at your house and in my garage. But eating—that's something he does *everywhere*. Yesterday we found out that he used to hang out at a pizzeria. And he often had lunch at Mr. Brown's. There are a few people like that around, just regular people who feed cats. But where is the most food *thrown out*?"

"Thrown out? At supermarkets, restaurants, butcher shops," Hillary said, after thinking a bit.

"Correct," said Kelly Ann. She tapped the open map on the table. "This is a map of Windsor, which belonged to my father, but he's given it to me. I drew this black line. It's the straightest route between your house and mine. *We* can't travel this way because of fences and large German shepherds. But M.C. can."

"So all we have to do is follow the black line to the counterfeiter, who will be eating in a restaurant?" Hillary said impatiently.

"I think M.C. would stick to as straight a route as possible between your house and mine," Kelly Ann said, ignoring Hillary's interruption. "But he stops along that route, because I got here yesterday from your house before he did."

Hillary nodded. Then her stomach made a squawking noise.

Kelly Ann jumped. "What's that?"

"I forgot," Hillary said sheepishly. She reached down and unhooked the walkie-talkie from her belt. She pulled out the antenna, turned up the volume, and heard, "Calling Hillary, calling Hillary. Come in, Hillary."

"Hi, Andrew," Hillary said into the walkie-talkie. "Can you hang on just a minute? We're not quite finished in here." She laid the walkie-talkie on the table.

Kelly Ann frowned. "What was I saying?"

"That M.C. got here yesterday after you did," Hillary prompted her.

"Oh, right. Since he left your house *before* I did, he obviously makes stops between your house and mine. And I think the stops he makes have to do with food. M.C. may have pulled the counterfeit bills out of a trash can. But I think he climbed into the trash can in the first place looking for something to eat."

Hillary fidgeted a little. "Are we ever coming to the point?" she wondered.

There was another squawk from the walkie-talkie. This time Kelly Ann picked it up. "Andrew," she said crossly, "we're busy!"

"Billy wants me to come over and play baseball," Andrew's voice said. "Can I?"

"Okay," Kelly Ann told him. "But stay away from nails."

She handed the walkie-talkie back to Hillary, who stuck it in her back pocket.

"This map," Kelly Ann went on in a louder voice—she realized she was losing her audience's attention—"is published by the Windsor Midtown Merchants' Association. On it are most of the stores—and restaurants—between our two houses. I think we should pick out the likeliest spots along the black line for M.C. to be climbing into trash cans. Then, after he's begun his rounds, we should go to some of those places and wait for him to show up."

"Like a stakeout," Hillary said slowly.

"Right," Kelly Ann resumed. "Instead of trying to tail M.C., which is impossible. And if he climbs into a trash can, we'll start taking a close look around for a counterfeiter."

Hillary looked down at the map. She didn't say anything.

"Do you think it's a dumb idea?" Kelly Ann asked.

"Actually," Hillary said admiringly, "it sounds like a very good idea."

A car door slammed outside.

Kelly Ann hastily folded up the Windsor merchants' map and stuck it in a drawer in the table. She was pretty certain that her mother wouldn't like the idea of her and Hillary tracking down a counterfeiter. So there was no sense in calling her attention to it.

Mrs. McCoy and Michael came into the kitchen, Michael proudly showing off the red welt on his arm. "That's the shot," he said to the girls.

"I'll bet you were brave," Hillary said.

"No, I cried," Michael answered truthfully. "Where's Andrew?"

"Playing baseball next door with Billy," Kelly Ann told him.

"Can I go, Mom?" Michael asked.

"'*May* I go,'" said his mother automatically. "Yes, go ahead. But be careful."

"It won't matter if I hurt myself," Michael said as he ran down the back steps, "because I've already had the shot for it."

Mrs. McCoy shook her head and smiled. "Would you like to have lunch with us, Hillary?" she asked.

"Actually, Mrs. McCoy," Hillary answered, "I asked Kelly Ann to eat lunch at my house."

"Well...if it won't be too much trouble for your mother," Mrs. McCoy said.

"Oh, no," Hillary answered. "Mrs. Griffis will help us."

"All right, then," Mrs. McCoy agreed.

"The map," Hillary whispered. "Don't forget the map."

"Hi, Mrs. Griffis," Hillary said to the housekeeper, who was in the kitchen. "Glynis around?"

"Hello, Mrs. Griffis," Kelly Ann echoed.

"Hello, girls," Mrs. Griffis answered. "Your mother said to go ahead with lunch and not to wait for her," Mrs. Griffis told Hillary. "She's stuck at a committee meeting. I'll be downstairs doing laundry. Call if you need help getting your lunch." She hurried down the basement stairs.

Hillary opened the refrigerator. "Better for

us," she said to Kelly Ann. "We can go over the plan."

Hillary took half a roast duck out of the refrigerator and started pulling it to pieces with her hands, being careful to discard any bones.

"Are we eating that?" Kelly Ann asked uncertainly.

Hillary laughed. "No, cold roast duck is too greasy for human consumption. This is for lazy old M.C. He climbed back into bed this morning after breakfast."

Hillary arranged the chunks of duck on a white porcelain plate and headed down the hall to her room, with Kelly Ann behind her.

The scruffy gray cat woke up when Hillary opened the door. "Mrow?" he said hopefully.

"That's right," Hillary said. "Grub."

She set the plate on the floor, and M.C. jumped down from the bed. He polished off the duck in seconds and looked around for more.

"That's all, you greedy thing," Hillary scolded.

M.C. licked his lips and sat down to wash his face. When he finished, Kelly Ann scratched the top of his head. M.C. closed his eyes in ecstasy.

"It's amazing, isn't it," Kelly Ann said, "that he eats all this stuff here and can still gobble down enormous bowls of cat food at my house?"

"And who knows what else in his travels?" Hillary added. "What's really amazing is, he's as bony as he ever was. George says he has a hollow leg." She picked the plate up off the floor. "Let's go eat something ourselves and take a good look at the map."

Hillary pulled assorted dishes out of the refrigerator and took a big loaf of bread off the counter. She carried them all to the dining room.

"Here's some silverware," she said to Kelly Ann, "and plates. Serve yourself—I'll bring the drinks."

Kelly Ann was making a salmon sandwich when Hillary put two glasses of soda on the table and sank down in her chair. "Ouch!" she said, standing up quickly. "What am I sitting on?"

It was the walkie-talkie she had stuck in her back pocket at the McCoys'. She laid it on the chair next to her. "You can take it with you when you go," she said to Kelly Ann.

But as they pored over the map, they forgot all about the walkie-talkie.

"This looks good," Hillary said, pointing to a group of little green squares representing stores and shops. "All in a pile—Right Way Supermarket, Burger Haven, and Chicken-to-Go."

"Let's put stars next to them," Kelly Ann suggested. "What about this? Side by side, Farley's Fish Market and Bronson's Selected Meats."

The girls picked out six or eight likely spots —"Enough to start with," Hillary said. "We'll get going as soon as M.C. does."

"I think we should make a pact," Kelly Ann told her. "We have to do our investigating together, okay? Counterfeiters probably don't have guns or anything, but two are still safer than one."

Hillary agreed. Then she hissed: "Put the map away, quick—here comes Glynis!"

"How are you, dear?" Mrs. Barnett greeted Kelly Ann. "Hillary, have you forgotten?"

"Huh?" said Hillary, looking blank.

"About your appointment at the orthodontist this afternoon," her mother said patiently.

"Oh, no!" moaned Hillary, smacking her forehead.

"We have to be there in half an hour," her mother reminded her.

"All right," Hillary said. "Let me go brush my teeth. Of all the rotten luck!" she said to Kelly Ann in a low voice. "Hey! There goes M.C.!"

The girls looked through the dining room window. The gray cat was purposefully cutting across the lawn on the other side of the street. He would crawl through the hedge, trample the pink lady's mimulus, and run along the stone wall above the German shepherd. Then he would be on his way to the trash cans behind Stan's Poultry Store. Or would he prefer the Fish Factory? And somewhere along the way was the counterfeiter.

"Of all the luck," Hillary repeated dejectedly.

"We'll do it tomorrow afternoon," Kelly Ann said.

Chapter Nine

The next day, M.C. abruptly changed his schedule. Maybe it was the weather: it was cool and cloudy and looked as if it might rain. Above all, M.C. hated getting wet.

Whatever it was, he took Hillary completely by surprise. She had slept late. Having her braces tightened by the orthodontist the day before had made her teeth ache, and she hadn't slept well. She was still lying in bed, reexamining Glynis's counterfeit ten-dollar bill and thinking about Kelly Ann's plan, when M.C. demanded to go out.

Puzzled, she pushed her window open. "Before your breakfast?" she said to M.C. "You're coming right back, aren't you?"

But when Hillary saw him stalk across the lawn and into the street, she knew he wasn't. "We can't miss another day!" she exclaimed, throwing on her clothes. "A counterfeiter isn't going to hang around forever!"

She picked up the phone on her night table and dialed Kelly Ann. "Maybe she can meet me somewhere along the way," Hillary reasoned to herself. But Kelly Ann's line was busy.

Hillary waited until she finished dressing and dialed again. Still busy! "I'll call her from a pay phone," she decided.

The evening before, she had found a copy of the Windsor Midtown Merchants' Association map in the kitchen. Now she stuck the map in her pocket. Hillary took some money out of her dresser drawer and jammed it into her other pocket. Then she stuffed the counterfeit ten in there, too—"For luck," she mumbled to herself.

Hillary raced through the house, stopping only to pick up the twins' walkie-talkie—she figured she'd end up at the McCoys' sooner or later.

"See you after awhile!" she yelled to Glynis, who was reading the morning paper in the living room. Then she dashed out the back door and jumped on her bike.

Hillary pulled the map out of her pocket and took a quick look at it. "M.C. might already be at the first stop—he could leave before I even get there. I'll try the next one," she decided. "I think that was the Fish Factory."

She folded the map and put it carefully away. Then she pedaled down her driveway at top speed and turned into the street.

"Hilldale, right on Waverly for six blocks. Left onto Shelby Road, then right again on Rivington." But when Hillary finally got there, she discovered that it had sounded more promising than it looked.

The Fish Factory was a dingy little store with a window full of tired-looking mackerel on ice and a few squid thrown in for variety. "Yuk!" she said. "M.C. must have better taste than this!"

There was a delicatessen a few doors down. And behind the row of nine or ten stores was an enormous open trash container with BARNEY'S SANITATION written on the side. Hillary stood on tiptoe and peered into it. Not that she expected the container to be full of counterfeit tens. "But you can never tell," she thought.

No funny money was in it that Hillary could see. There *were* a bunch of chicken necks and some fish heads. This was definitely a possibility for one of M.C.'s snacks.

M.C. was still nowhere in sight. Now was a good time to try Kelly Ann again. There were two pay phones on the corner. Hillary dropped a quarter in the first one: it was out of order. And it kept her money.

She tried the second, waiting for a dial tone and then dialing Kelly Ann's number. The McCoys' line was still busy!

Hillary slammed down the phone, thoroughly exasperated. Again her money wasn't returned. She pushed down the handle for coin release, but still nothing happened.

"Wonderful!" Hillary muttered. "That was the last of my change. Now I'll have to try to get change in one of those stores."

First she went into a shop that sold magazines, newspapers, and candy. "Sorry," the man behind the counter said primly, "I can only give you change if you purchase something."

Hillary looked around for something to buy. But most of the magazines were old and the candy seemed even older. She walked outside again and glanced down the row of shops.

Her eye was caught by a huge black-and-white poster of a poodle. It was about two and a half feet by three and a half feet, so big that every one of the dog's whiskers showed up clearly. Next to it was a handwritten sign: "Photos made poster size for only $4.95."

Hillary tried to imagine a photo of M.C. that large: one good ear and one notched ear, his crooked tail—and he might even be showing his sandpaper tongue and still-spotless teeth.

Hillary grinned. Maybe she'd have one made for herself and one for Kelly Ann. She took a last look around the parking lot for M.C. It was starting to drizzle a little.

"He'll probably hole up somewhere until the rain stops," Hillary decided.

She stepped inside the door of the shop with the poodle poster. The name of the store was Quick Print. There were a couple of battered copiers in the back of the room. A wrinkled price list, and samples of printed stationery and restaurant menus hung from a bulletin board.

Hillary walked up to the counter, where a young woman with long hair was reading a newspaper. "Excuse me," Hillary said. "I'm interested in having a poster made. Does there have to be anything special about the photograph?"

"Naw," the young woman answered, stifling a yawn. "Glossy is better than matte finish, black-and-white better than color. But anything'll do."

"Okay, thanks," Hillary said. Then she remembered she needed change. She pulled a bill out of her pocket and held it in front of the woman's sleepy eyes. "Could you change this for me?" she asked.

Hillary's mind was still on the poster, so she didn't really look at the bill she handed the woman. And Hillary didn't notice the woman draw in her breath when *she* saw the bill. The woman's eyes narrowed as she took it.

"Sure," the young woman drawled. "But you'll have to wait a minute. My change drawer is still downstairs—I just opened up." As if it were an afterthought, she added, "Want to come down and see how I do the posters?"

"Sure," Hillary said. She slipped under the high counter and followed the woman through a door on a side wall.

The woman flipped a light switch. "Right down there," she told Hillary, pointing to a steep flight of stairs. Hillary hadn't walked down more than three steps when the woman called out harshly. "Barry! I warned you to burn those bills!"

As Hillary turned around, she saw the woman close the door and turn the lock.

Chapter Ten

A t first Hillary didn't understand what was going on. She turned around to look at the woman behind her. But the woman's eyes were on someone downstairs.

"I did burn them, Carol!" growled a burly man with a mustache. "Who's the kid?"

"I guess she thought she was being cute," Carol said, giving Hillary a shove. "Look what she just brought in—for change, she said." At the bottom of the stairs she took Hillary by the arm and pulled her none too gently toward the man named Barry. Then she handed Barry the bill Hillary had given her.

"Glynis's counterfeit ten, for luck!" Hillary thought, horrified. "Some luck!" Kelly Ann's plan had worked, all too well—Hillary had found the counterfeiter!

"You obviously didn't burn *all* of them," sneered Carol. "Doesn't that look familiar?"

Barry turned the ten over. "Yeah, it's one of the test bills, all right. But where'd she get it?" He glared at Hillary. "Where'd you get it, kid?"

"It's...it's my allowance," Hillary stammered

feebly. "It's my weekly allowance."

"Yeah, sure," Barry said. "Probably found it out back—I *could* have missed one or two of 'em." He stepped closer to Hillary.

"What difference does it make?" Carol snapped. "The question is, what are we going to do about it?"

"Well," Barry said, frowning, "we'll have to get her out of the way, at least until I'm finished here. I'm right in the middle of the last run, and they're looking real good."

Get her out of the way? Hillary had never been so scared in her life! Why hadn't she waited for Kelly Ann? "Two are safer than one." She could almost hear Kelly Ann saying it.

"I don't know what you're talking about," Hillary said to Carol and Barry. "Why don't you show me the posters, and then I'll go home?"

Carol just stared at her. "Cute," she said with an unfriendly smile. "Very cute."

"I've gotta get back to the press," Barry said. For the first time, Hillary's ears registered a clacking sound coming from another basement room.

"And I've got to go back upstairs and try to make this place look like a legitimate business," Carol retorted. "So what about her?"

"Oh, who cares," Barry answered vaguely. "Stuff her in the closet until we're ready to leave."

"Into the other room," Carol ordered Hillary. "Quick!"

There was the printing press, clicking and clacking away in the center of a small, cluttered room. Out of the corner of her eye, Hillary saw one of the printed sheets of paper that came rolling off the cylinders. On the sheet were the green backs of six ten-dollar bills: three above and three below.

She didn't have time to get more than a glimpse. Carol pointed toward the half-open door of a narrow closet. "In there," she said sharply. When Hillary hesitated, Carol gave her a shove.

Hillary stepped into the closet and turned around. High on the opposite wall of the room she saw two windows, but the glass in them had been painted black. The Carol slammed the door in her face.

Hillary heard Carol snap shut the padlock on the outside. And she could hear her tell Barry, "I'm going back upstairs."

"Mmmm," Barry grunted.

Then there was silence, except for the clickety-clacking of the press turning out thousands of dollars' worth of counterfeit bills. Hillary sat down on a box. What was she going to do?

"It's roasting in here," Barry grumbled. There was the sound of him opening one of the windows a little.

The closet was warm and very stuffy. "No one is ever going to find me in here, because no one knows where I went," Hillary thought. "What if they leave me in here for days? I could suffocate! Or starve!" Her stomach growled complainingly.

She tried to calm down. She wiped the perspiration off her forehead with her hand and wiped her hand on her shorts. It brushed against something on her belt—the twins' walkie-talkie!

How was that going to help her? Hillary was sure it wouldn't work over a long range. Even if it could, the chances of Andrew or Michael switching on a single walkie-talkie. . .what would be the point? Besides, was Barry going to stand there and let her call in rescuers?

Still, Hillary was kind of glad she had it. It made her feel a little less alone. She unhooked the walkie-talkie from her belt, stuck it in her back pocket, and pulled her shirttail down over it. They weren't going to take it away from her if she could help it.

"How did *you* get in here!" Barry roared suddenly on the other side of the door.

Hillary flinched. But he didn't mean *her.*

"Dumb cat!" Barry muttered. Hillary could hear him moving quickly around the room, knocking into things as he went.

Cat? Could it be M.C.?

"M.C.!" Hillary shouted.

"Mrow?" she heard.

Then there was a terrific crash, followed by

another, and a terrible, piercing yowl. What had Barry done to M.C.?

"You leave him alone!" Hillary screamed.

"What's going on down here?" Carol's voice demanded.

"Stupid cat—must have jumped through the window. He turned over some of the ink!" Barry said angrily. "And scratched me good!"

"Poor baby!" Carol said sarcastically. "*What* cat?"

"I hit him with a board and threw him out the window," Barry answered.

"Keep the windows closed. And try to keep it quiet down here!"

"Yeah," Barry said. He stomped over to the closet. "If you make any more noise," he said to Hillary through the door, "I'll make you very sorry."

Hillary didn't say anything. She was sure it had been M.C. in the basement. And from the sound he had made, she *knew* he was hurt. She just didn't know how badly. Tears welled up in her eyes.

Chapter Eleven

It had been a hectic day at the McCoys', and it wasn't even half over. Mr. McCoy had gotten a phone call very early that morning about a big job. He had raced out of the house in the middle of breakfast. The twins had a birthday party to go to at Tommy Larson's, which involved brunch and an early movie. They had had to be bathed, combed, and dressed, and their present wrapped, all before ten o'clock. Then Mrs. McCoy's car wouldn't start, so Kelly Ann had to sit in it and press down the gas pedal while her mother fiddled under the hood and the twins complained about being late.

Finally, everyone had left the house except Kelly Ann. She sighed happily and reached for the telephone, only to discover that it was off the hook. So the phone probably hadn't been working since her father had gotten his early-morning call. What if Hillary had been trying to get her?

Kelly Ann hung up the phone, then picked it up again and hurriedly dialed the Barnetts' number. It rang and rang. She was about to give up when Mrs. Griffis answered, out of breath.

"Hi, Mrs. Griffis. Is Hillary there?" Kelly Ann asked.

"Nobody's here. I knocked good and loud, and nobody opened the door. Finally had to let myself in," Mrs. Griffis puffed.

"Do you know where Hillary could have gone?"

"No idea," Mrs. Griffis said, "since I just got here myself. Maybe she's on her way to your house."

"Thanks," Kelly Ann said and hung up.

She went outside to wait for Hillary to turn into the driveway. It was starting to drizzle out, so she sat down on the couch in the living room and stared out the front window for half an hour. But Hillary didn't show up.

Kelly Ann dialed the Barnetts' again. Maybe Hillary had gone on an errand with her mother and was back home now.

This time Mrs. Barnett answered the phone. "She left early this morning," Mrs. Barnett told Kelly Ann. "I thought she was with you."

"Did she say anything when she left?" Kelly Ann asked.

"No," Mrs. Barnett answered. "Just that she'd see me after a while. Would you please have her call me if she comes to your house?"

Kelly Ann had one more question: "Is M.C. around?"

"I haven't seen him," Mrs. Barnett said.

Where could Hillary have gone? If they hadn't made a pact, Kelly Ann might have thought Hillary was out tracking down the counterfeiter alone. But hadn't they agreed, "two are safer than one"?

Kelly Ann couldn't sit still any longer. She went to her room and took her yellow slicker out of the closet. "I'll ride my bike toward Hillary's house," she decided. "Maybe I'll run into her halfway."

Kelly Ann took the Windsor merchants' map with her—perhaps she'd have a quick look around a few of the spots they'd picked to stake out. Sometimes Hillary rushed into things.

Now it was drizzling steadily. Because of the rain, there weren't many people on the streets. Kelly Ann checked out Charlie's Chicken Coop. But she didn't see Hillary.

Or M.C. . . . until she had ridden back and was turning into her own street. Then she saw him moving slowly along the edge of the road instead of cutting unconcernedly across lawns the way he usually did.

M.C. was limping. "He's hurt!" Kelly Ann cried out. She braked to a stop across the street from the big gray cat.

M.C. raised his head to look at Kelly Ann. "Miou?" he said plaintively.

"M.C., what's happened to you?" Kelly Ann gasped, kneeling down next to him in the rain.

He had a swelling over one eye the size of a walnut. And there was a deep gash on his left hip —blood was oozing out of it.

Kelly Ann pushed her bike up onto a neighbor's lawn. Then she unzipped her slicker and took it off. She wrapped it gently around M.C. and carefully picked him up.

"Mrow," he said and started to purr—Kelly Ann could feel it through the slicker. She walked as fast as she could toward her house.

Mrs. McCoy must have seen her coming, because she was waiting in the front yard with an umbrella when Kelly Ann got there. "Kelly Ann, you're soaked!" she exclaimed.

"M.C.'s hurt," Kelly Ann said stiffly, trying not to cry.

"Give him to me while you go back for your bike," Mrs. McCoy directed.

When Kelly Ann got back to the house, her mother had already set M.C. down on the rug in the living room and peeled away the yellow slicker.

"Let's have a look at you," Mrs. McCoy said to the bedraggled gray cat. She ran her fingers lightly over the huge bump on his head. "Just missed his eye," she murmured. "I think it's okay —just swollen," she said to Kelly Ann. But when she saw the deep gash she said, "Mmmm. That should probably be stitched up. I'd better call Dr. Lufrano." Dr. Lufrano was Samantha's vet.

Mrs. McCoy was soon back. "She said to bring him right in," she told Kelly Ann.

She helped her daughter get M.C. out to the car. The car actually started, first time. "*Someone* is on M.C.'s side," Mrs. McCoy said.

M.C. didn't like his second ride to the vet any better than he had liked his first, with the Barnetts. But Kelly Ann managed to keep him quiet, and with her mother's help was able to bundle him into the vet's office.

"I don't think it's serious," Dr. Lufrano reassured Kelly Ann. "But I do have to sew up the gash on his hip. He has to have an anesthetic, so you'll have to leave him here until later this afternoon. You can pick him up around two-thirty," she told Kelly Ann's mother.

"You'd better let Hillary know," Mrs. McCoy said as they walked through the rain to the car.

"I don't know where she is," Kelly Ann answered.

Back home, Kelly Ann dialed the Barnetts' again. Mrs. Barnett answered the phone. "Did you hear from Hillary?" she asked anxiously, before Kelly Ann could ask her anything.

When Kelly Ann said no, Mrs. Barnett told her, "I'm beginning to get a little worried. I wonder if I should telephone. . .Thank you for calling, Kelly Ann," she said distractedly. "Good-bye."

Chapter Twelve

For what seemed like a long time, Hillary hadn't heard anything but the clacking of what she had begun to think of as the "funny-money machine." Like the noise of a train clicking along the tracks, it was an oddly soothing sound. It was so warm in the closet. Hillary was suddenly exhausted. Her eyes felt heavy. She dozed off.

Hillary awakened with a start. She had been dreaming about being asleep at home in bed, with M.C. lying on his pillow at her feet. When she woke up sitting on a box in a cramped closet, she didn't understand where she was for a second. But just for a second, because someone rapped on the closet door and growled, "Still with us, kid?" It was Barry. Hillary remembered everything.

"Yes," she said through clenched teeth.

"Good." Barry chuckled unpleasantly.

Then Hillary heard him talking to Carol. "We're almost done," he said.

"We should go back to the apartment and pack up our stuff," Carol said. "People are going to start poking around, looking for the kid. We'd better get ready to move."

"Yeah," Barry agreed. "We'll trim the bills, pack the plates, and get out of here." He paused. "I've been thinking—maybe we'll take the kid with us."

Hillary's heart stopped.

"To California?" Carol screeched.

"Naw!" Barry grunted. "We'll put her out on the turnpike three or four hundred miles down the road. It'll give us a good start before anyone finds her."

"I could handle that," Hillary thought bravely. But what if they changed their minds? They could decide to take her a lot farther than that, or even get rid of her altogether.

"That's it!" Barry announced suddenly. "Finished." The clacking of the press stopped abruptly.

"Great!" Carol said.

Barry clumped over the the closet. "Make any noise at all, kid," he threatened, "and you're doomed."

Then Hillary heard them tramping up the stairs. A door slammed overhead. Barry and Carol were gone.

Hillary rattled the closet door. It was still padlocked, of course. Then she braced her back against the back wall of the closet and pushed against the door with both feet—it didn't budge.

Hillary was afraid to scream for help. What if the counterfeiters heard her? She took the twins' walkie-talkie out of her back pocket. She pulled out the antenna and flicked the switch on the side.

"Calling anybody, calling anybody," she said urgently. "This is Hillary. Come in, please."

Hillary didn't have great hopes, but at least it gave her the feeling she was doing something to get herself out of this mess. She would keep it up until someone heard her, or the batteries ran down, or Barry and Carol came back.

Mrs. McCoy was ladling some soup into a bowl for Kelly Ann when she caught sight of her daughter's face. "You don't have to look so worried," she said. "M.C.'s going to be fine."

Kelly Ann shook her head. "It's not that," she answered. "It's Hillary."

Then she told her mother the whole story: starting with the two counterfeit bills and M.C.'s reputation as a crime-buster, and ending with the plan she had come up with for a feline stakeout.

"What if Hillary tried the plan alone and something happened to her?" Kelly Ann said anxiously. "It would be all my fault."

"Kelly Ann, I'm sure it's a very good plan," her mother said. "But there's a strong possibility that the counterfeiter is no longer in Windsor. Maybe a store owner was passed the bills, then threw them out when he realized what they were. And if there *were* counterfeiters around, I'm sure Hillary wouldn't try anything dangerous. She's too sensible for that."

Kelly Ann seemed doubtful.

"I'm sure of it," Mrs. McCoy repeated. "Look —it's raining. Maybe Hillary rode her bike to the mall to walk around. Or went to an early movie, like the twins."

Kelly Ann nodded. She would have liked to believe that, but then why hadn't Hillary called her?

"Sit down and eat your lunch," Mrs. McCoy said. "It'll be time to pick up M.C.—and the twins —before you know it."

First Kelly Ann and her mother stopped for the twins at the birthday party. They came racing out of the house when they saw the car. Michael had spilled pink punch all down the front of his new shirt. One of the pockets of Andrew's pants was torn halfway off.

"It looks as though it was a successful party," Mrs. McCoy murmured to Kelly Ann.

"It was great!" Andrew said, climbing into the back seat. "Look what we got!" He poked a blue rubber dinosaur into the front seat.

"Yeah, look!" Michael added, shoving a toothy brownish one at his mother.

"Wait a minute!" Mrs. Larson waved and ran

through the rain holding a walkie-talkie. "Andrew forgot this!" she explained to Mrs. McCoy.

"What were you going to do with *one* walkie-talkie?" Kelly Ann asked her brother as they drove away.

"I wanted to show it to the guys. I thought if Tommy got a set for his birthday, we could all talk," Andrew answered. He pulled the antenna up, turned the walkie-talkie on, and spoke into it: "Calling Hillary, calling Hillary."

"Why Hillary?" his mother asked, looking at Andrew in the rearview mirror.

"Because she's got mine," Michael said sensibly.

"Where are we going?" asked Andrew.

"To pick up M.C. at the vet's," Kelly Ann said.

"What's the matter with him?" Michael asked.

"He was in an accident," Mrs. McCoy told him. "He had to have some stitches."

"And a shot?" Michael asked, touching his arm.

"Probably," his mother said. "Here we are. Do you boys want to come in or wait in the car?"

The memory of his own shot was still too fresh. "Wait in the car," Michael said, clutching his dinosaur.

"Me, too," said Andrew. "Calling Hillary, calling Hillary," he said into his walkie-talkie.

Dr. Lufrano lifted M.C. out of a cage and laid

him on the examination table. The gray cat raised a heavy head and mewed sleepily.

"I took three stitches in his hip," Dr. Lufrano told Kelly Ann. M.C.'s hair had been shaved around the deep cut, and Kelly Ann could see three neat stitches taken with black thread that pulled the skin together.

"And I x-rayed his head—it's fine," the vet went on. "It will just take awhile for the swelling to go down. I've also given him a tetanus shot, just to be on the safe side." She gave M.C. a pat. "Do you have any idea what happened to him?"

"No," Kelly Ann answered. "When I found him, he was trying to get to my house."

"When I cleaned around the wound, I found green paint on his fur. Or ink," Dr. Lufrano said.

She scooped M.C. up and handed him to Kelly Ann. "He's still very groggy. Keep him inside"—Kelly Ann looked at her mother—"and quiet. Don't let him jump up on anything until the anesthetic wears off."

"Why don't you take M.C. out to the car while I write Dr. Lufrano a check?" Mrs. McCoy said to her daughter.

"Open the door!" Kelly Ann yelled at her brothers in the closed car. Her hands were full of Mystery Cat—and she was getting wet.

Michael leaned over the front seat, pulled the handle on the car door, and shoved it open. Kelly Ann slid onto the seat and put M.C. carefully

down next to her. Then she closed the door.

"Guess what? Guess what?" the twins were shouting.

"Sssssh!" Kelly Ann warned, making sure M.C. didn't jump up. "What?"

"We talked to Hillary!" Andrew said.

"What!" Kelly Ann shrieked. "What do you mean?"

"On the walkie-talkie. Listen!" Andrew handed the walkie-talkie to Kelly Ann.

At first she heard only the crackle of static. Then she heard a voice, very faint: "It's Hillary ...closet...counterfeit..."

"Hillary!" Kelly Ann screamed into the walkie-talkie. "Where are you?"

"...trapped...closet...M.C." the tiny voice said. Then there was static again.

"Why isn't it working?!" Kelly Ann said frantically. "Andrew, make it work!"

Andrew flicked the switch on and off a few times. He tapped the walkie-talkie against the car door. But Hillary's voice was gone.

"I guess she's switched hers off," Andrew told Kelly Ann.

Hillary knocked her walkie-talkie against the closet doorknob. It was dead—the batteries had finally run down. But she was overjoyed.

"They heard me!" she said ecstatically. "The McCoys actually *heard* me!"

Chapter Thirteen

"She said something about the counterfeiter. And that she was trapped in a closet." Kelly Ann took a deep breath, having just told everything to Sergeant Thomas at the Windsor Police Station.

"Mrs. Barnett called us earlier," the sergeant told Mrs. McCoy. "But we felt it was too soon to worry, that Hillary would turn up on her own. It looks as though we were wrong." Then he asked, "Do you know what the range of your sons' walkie-talkie is?"

"No, I'm afraid I don't," Mrs. McCoy said apologetically. "My husband might know."

"I know!" Andrew spoke up. "Longest range is one-half mile."

"Good for you!" Sergeant Thomas beamed at Andrew. "Now, where were you exactly when you heard Hillary's voice?"

"At the doctor's," Michael said.

"The veterinarian—on the corner of Oak and Glendale," Mrs. McCoy told the sergeant.

Sergeant Thomas rummaged through a drawer of his desk until he found a compass.

Then he stepped quickly over to a large map of Windsor Township hanging on the wall. He adjusted the compass to a scale of half a mile. He put the point of the compass on the corner where Dr. Lufrano's office was and drew a circle in pencil on the map.

"Your friend is somewhere inside this circle," he said to Kelly Ann. "Do you think you can narrow it down a little more?"

"Maybe I have..." Kelly Ann dug into the deep pocket of her slicker and pulled out the Windsor merchants' map. "Yes—we marked all the likely spots with stars," she said, handing the map to Sergeant Thomas.

"Likely spots for the counterfeiter to be?" asked the sergeant.

Kelly Ann nodded. "Or, really, likely spots for our cat, M.C., to climb into trash cans," she added for accuracy's sake.

The sergeant compared Kelly Ann's map with the map on the wall. "Two of your likely spots fall within this circle," he said. "Bronson's Selected Meats and the Fish Factory."

He stuck his head into the squad room: "Haney, Gertz. We're going to take a look at Bronson's on Oak, and the Fish Factory on Rivington, for the Barnett girl. Bronson's first."

Sergeant Thomas turned back to the McCoys and said, "I can't fit all of you into my car. But I'd like to take Kelly Ann along—she knows Hillary so well that she may be helpful in finding her."

"Go ahead," Kelly Ann's mother told her. "We'll be keeping M.C. company until you get back."

The sergeant's blue-and-white sedan sped silently through the rainy streets, the other two policemen in the car behind it. "No sirens," Sergeant Thomas explained to Kelly Ann. "We don't want to alert anyone that we're coming."

He pulled up at the edge of the parking lot behind Bronson's. He climbed out of the car to talk to the patrolmen. Then he sat down with Kelly Ann again, while the other men walked over to the butcher shop.

They came out right away. They were in and out of the remaining stores very quickly, too.

"Nothing here," Haney reported.

"Then let's go to the Fish Factory," Sergeant Thomas said. "Step on it!"

"I don't know," he said doubtfully when he saw the single row of dingy little shops. But the sergeant motioned the two patrolmen forward, then climbed out of his own car.

Kelly could see him talking to the clerk on the other side of the grimy plate-glass window of the Fish Factory. The man was looking down at the floor as if he were thinking. Then he shook his head. The sergeant spoke again. The man shook his head again.

Sergeant Thomas left the fish store and

joined the patrolmen outside. They tried the door of a shop with a poster in the window. But the door was locked, and the lights inside the store were turned off. Quick Print was closed.

Then the three policemen went into a shop that sold candy and newspapers. This time they didn't come right back out. Kelly Ann wondered what was going on.

Suddenly Sergeant Thomas pushed open the door and walked quickly back to the car. "We may have something here," he told Kelly Ann. "The man in the newsstand said a girl came in this morning to ask if he could change a bill for her—all he remembers is she had dark hair."

"Hillary does," Kelly Ann said.

The sergeant nodded. "Her mother described her when she called. Sit tight," he told Kelly Ann. "We're going to take a look around back."

The three policemen walked around the side of the newspaper store and disappeared from view. But Sergeant Thomas was back almost immediately, pushing a bike in front of him.

"That's Hillary's!" said Kelly Ann.

"I found it leaning against a trash container," the sergeant said. "And didn't you mention something about green paint on your cat?"

"Yes—or ink," Kelly Ann answered.

"We've just found a trail of green cat prints leading away from a basement window," he told

Kelly Ann, "in back of Quick Print. We're going in!"

In the closet in the basement of Quick Print, Hillary had gotten over her excitement about contacting the McCoys. "There's no way they'll find me in time," she thought resignedly. She tried to keep her spirits up: "I'll act dumb and cooperate. Maybe Barry and Carol will let me out before they get to California." But she was feeling pretty discouraged.

That's when she heard the glass breaking. Was Barry back? Had he dropped something?

Then a loud voice called out: "Police! Is anybody down there?"

"Here I am!" Hillary screamed. "I'm locked in the closet!"

Officer Haney broke the rest of the glass out of the small window. Then Sergeant Thomas and Officer Gertz lowered him through it into the basement of Quick Print.

"I'll have you out of there in a minute," he told Hillary through the closet door. It looked too solid to kick in. He used his pocketknife to unscrew the hinges. Finally, Hillary was free!

"Wow! Thanks!" Hillary exclaimed. She looked apprehensively at the stairs. "The counterfeiters'll probably be back any minute," she said a little nervously.

"Let's get you out of here," Officer Haney

said. "And don't worry about the counterfeiters—we'll take care of them."

He pushed an old bookcase under the window and helped Hillary climb up on it. Then Sergeant Thomas grabbed her arms and pulled her through the window.

"Hillary Barnett?" the sergeant asked.

Hillary nodded.

"You've had quite a time of it, haven't you?" the sergeant said.

"Oh, it wasn't too bad," Hillary answered pluckily.

But when Kelly Ann jumped out of the police car and gave her a big hug, Hillary cried, just a little. "How embarrassing," she said, hastily wiping away her tears. "It's just that I'm kind of relieved. I thought Barry and Carol would be dragging me to California—the counterfeiters," she added, seeing Kelly Ann's puzzled expression. "But you found me!"

Hillary handed Kelly Ann the walkie-talkie. "I'll have to buy the twins some new batteries," she said with a grin. "If it weren't for this, who knows what would have happened."

"This and M.C.," Kelly Ann said. "His green footprints led Sergeant Thomas right to the basement window."

"M.C.!" Hillary had been afraid to ask about him. "Is—is he okay? There were some awful crashes, and he made such a terrible sound, I thought . . ."

"No," Kelly Ann said quickly. "A big lump on his head and three stitches on his back leg, but he didn't use up even *one* of his nine lives. In fact, he's at the police station right now with Mom and the twins."

Sergeant Thomas came back to the car. "The counterfeiters will have quite a surprise waiting for them," he told the girls. Then he radioed for another police car. And he asked the dispatcher to phone Mrs. Barnett to tell her that Hillary had been found and was fine.

"Now I'm going to get you both back to the station," the sergeant said. He loaded Hillary's bike into the trunk.

"What happens now?" Hillary asked on the way to the Windsor Police Station. "To Barry and Carol, I mean."

"Counterfeiting comes under the jurisdiction of the United States Secret Service," Sergeant Thomas explained. "They'll take charge of the counterfeit bills and the printing plates—and the counterfeiters as well." He turned to look at Hillary and Kelly Ann. "You may even get a citation from the U.S. Department of the Treasury for your help."

"It's M.C. who should get the citation," Hillary said. "He's the one who put us on to it. And the one who got me out of it. I guess the Mystery Cat hasn't lost his touch."

Chapter Fourteen

The girls were sitting on the McCoys' back steps with Samantha at their feet.

"So, what are you going to do until you go to camp?" Kelly Ann asked Hillary.

"I've had enough excitement for *ten* summers," Hillary answered. "For the next few weeks I'm going to do nothing, just nothing."

"What'll happen to your half of M.C. while you're away?" Kelly Ann asked.

"Glynis is so happy he found me that *she's* going to feed him. She's even talking about having a cat door built, so M.C. can come in and out whenever he wants," Hillary said with a grin.

"Hey, Kelly Ann! Hillary!" the twins shouted from the other side of the house. "M.C.'s here—and he's got something *interesting* in his mouth."

In an instant the girls were on their feet.

"Oh, no!" Kelly Ann said.

"My thought exactly!" said Hillary. "How about a bike ride?"

They were down the driveway and out into the street before anyone could say "Mystery Cat."

About the Author

Susan Saunders was born in San Antonio, Texas. After earning a B.A. from Barnard College in New York City, she began a career in publishing. She worked as an editor, writer, and designer for several major film companies and publishing houses.

Four years ago, Ms. Saunders left her position as editor to write full-time. She is the author of over twenty children's books, of which two were Junior Literary Guild selections, one a Book-of-the-Month Club Dragon Magic selection, and one a Notable Children's Trade Book chosen by the National Council for the Social Studies/ Children's Book Council Joint Committee.

Ms. Saunders lives on Manhattan's Upper West Side, where she cohabits with a Cairn terrier and three rambunctious cats.

About the Illustrator

Eileen Christelow is an author, artist, and professional photographer who lives in Marlboro, Vermont, with her husband, their daughter, and a cat named Maude.